Cheaters

Michael Jacobs

SAMUEL FRENCH

FOUNDED 1830

SAMUELFRENCH.COM
SAMUELFRENCH-LONDON.CO.UK

FOR PRODUCTION ENQUIRIES

UNITED STATES AND CANADA
Info@SamuelFrench.com
1-866-598-8449

UNITED KINGDOM AND EUROPE
Theatre@SamuelFrench-London.co.uk
020-7255-4302

Each title is subject to availability from Samuel French, depending
upon country of performance. Please be aware that *CHEATERS* may
not be licensed by Samuel French in your territory. Professional and
amateur producers should contact the nearest Samuel French office or
licensing partner to verify availability.

MUSIC USE NOTE

Licensees are solely responsible for obtaining formal written permission from copyright owners to use copyrighted music in the performance of this play and are strongly cautioned to do so. If no such permission is obtained by the licensee, then the licensee must use only original music that the licensee owns and controls. Licensees are solely responsible and liable for all music clearances and shall indemnify the copyright owners of the play(s) and their licensing agent, Samuel French, against any costs, expenses, losses and liabilities arising from the use of music by licensees. Please contact the appropriate music licensing authority in your territory for the rights to any incidental music.

IMPORTANT BILLING AND CREDIT REQUIREMENTS

If you have obtained performance rights to this title, please refer to your licensing agreement for important billing and credit requirements.

CHEATERS was first produced on Broadway at the Biltmore Theatre in New York City on January 15, 1978. It was produced by Kenneth Marsolais, Philip Getter, and Leonard Soloway. The performance was directed by Robert Drivas, with sets by Lawrence King, costumes, by Jane Greenwood, and lighting by Ian Calderon. The Production Stage Manager was Larry Forde. The cast was as follows:

MONICA . . . . Rosemary Murphy

HOWARD . . . . Lou Jacobi

SAM . . . . Jack Weston

GRACE . . . . Doris Roberts

MICHELLE . . . . Roxanne Hart

ALLEN . . . . Jim Staskel

CHARACTERS

MONICA

HOWARD

SAM

GRACE

MICHELLE

ALLEN

SETTING

Act I

Rooms in New York City and Union, New Jersey; homes in Larchmont,
New York, and Englewood, New Jersey.

Act II

The home in Englewood, New Jersey.

For my Father.

ACT ONE

SCENE ONE

(HOWARD *and* MONICA)

(*A New York City bedroom – evening*)

(HOWARD, *fifties, sitting up in bed, fully dressed, shoes on, reading the* Times. MONICA, *unsettled with fifty, propped up on an elbow next to him, in a silk robe.*)

MONICA. I'm naked under this.

HOWARD. I'll take that under consideration.

MONICA. (*pulls the robe off of her shoulder*) What do you consider when I do this?

HOWARD. (*watches her*) When you do that I think about how when the robe comes off there's just going to be so much work.

MONICA. (*smiles*) Howard, why is it that when I'm not in the mood, you regard it as a personal attack?

HOWARD. (*looking at newspaper*) We have a very precarious world situation!

MONICA. But when you're not in the mood I should just live without it.

HOWARD. (*looks at her*) You can't live without it?

MONICA. I can't. Because you have always played my body like it was a violin, and you were a clarinet player, who doesn't know how to play the violin.

HOWARD. Stop pressuring me with your availability.

MONICA. (*regards him*) Are you just having fun raising the stakes of the conversation or do we have some trouble here?

HOWARD. I meant no conversation. I was counting on the world situation to keep us from having a conversation. I mean, there's just so much destructive capability. Somebody *USE* something!

MONICA. Are you hoping the world ends so you don't have to talk to me?

HOWARD. *(irritated)* But it *WON'T* end. It hasn't ended since I *MET* you.

(MONICA considers her options.)

MONICA. Relationships go through this. I think within the natural arc of a relationship there are moments when a person wishes there was a button to push that could make the other person go away for a while.

HOWARD. *(intrigued)* You mean cease to exist?

MONICA. No, the other person would still exist.

HOWARD. Okay, well I would be interested in purchasing the button next to that one.

MONICA. I'm trying to let you know that I possess enough sophistication to understand how even two people who have shared intimacy, could sometimes –

HOWARD. *(puts up a finger)* Immediately after the intimacy –

MONICA. Want the other person to –

HOWARD. *(uses the finger to push a button)* Cease to exist.

MONICA. No.

HOWARD. Never to have existed before or after the intimacy, and during the intimacy to have been somebody else.

MONICA. *(snaps)* No! What the hell happened to us?

HOWARD. I don't know, Monica. *(takes her hands)* But when you think about it, I can get this same thing at home with my wife.

MONICA. Then why are you holding my hands?

HOWARD. Because I don't want to get hit.

MONICA. *(pulls away from him)* Don't talk about your wife when you're here with me.

HOWARD. You're upset with my wife now? My wife is a *saint!*

MONICA. The hell with your wife.

HOWARD. Don't you *DARE!* My wife's name has no business coming out of that *mouth!*

MONICA. Mrs. Howard Janowitz.

HOWARD. *SAINT!*

(**MONICA** *turns around and wags her ass at him.*)

MONICA. Mrs. Howard Janowitz.

(**HOWARD**, *flustered, by reflex, slaps her ass.*)

MONICA. Now, we're talkin'.

(**HOWARD** *pulls his hand back immediately, and holds them both up, away from her.*)

HOWARD. No.

MONICA. You can't turn this down.

HOWARD. *(resolved)* I'm-a-turnin'-it-down!

MONICA. *(stung)* Then…that's it.

HOWARD. No, *you* don't say "that's it"! That's what *I've* been saying is it! I am officially calling this whole situation.

(*He picks up the clock on the night stand.*)

Time of death of this relationship; nine-forty-two.

(**MONICA** *realizes that he is actually breaking-up with her.*)

MONICA. Howard, we've been together eight months. This is not the way you do this.

(*He absorbs that.*)

HOWARD. You're right. There have to be words. We should explore feelings.

MONICA. I would love to explore your feelings.

HOWARD. No, the window closed on that.

MONICA. When?

HOWARD. As soon as I said it I knew I wasn't doing it. But I'll give you this: I am genuinely torn and bewildered by how the shared intimacy we had on that first night could take me eight months to get out of. *(backs toward the door)* And so goodbye.

MONICA. Hey! *Nobody walks out on me!*

    (HOWARD stops, amused.)

HOWARD. Did you just actually say that?

MONICA. Yeah, because how often does the chance come up?

HOWARD. Well, you delivered the hell out of it.

MONICA. *(nods, pleased)* I did, didn't I? *(then)* Could you please at least tell me what happened to us?

HOWARD. *(sighs)* Ahh, Monica, you said it best. Within the natural arc of this relationship I was intrigued by you, I was less intrigued by you and now I want you not to be alive. But I am very impressed with you for not being too terribly angry.

MONICA. *(calmly)* Oh, but I am terribly angry.

HOWARD. Really? Because you're not exhibiting the classic signs.

MONICA. Because that kind of anger rises up real fast and goes away. This is a far more dangerous anger that will consume me and get me started on my new project.

HOWARD. Well, I'm sure that has nothing to do with me, so what I'm going to do, is – *(He extends his arm and points to the door.)*

MONICA. Because it's all very amusing, your ideas of how, in your perfect world, you would be able to take what you want from someone and then treat them as though they had never been. But what you might find less amusing is that if you walk out the door, I'm going to dedicate some time to figure out how to actually kill you and get away with it.

HOWARD. *(impressed) Really?*

MONICA. *(resolved)* Yeah, because I've done everything else.

(HOWARD looks at her and mulls that over.)

HOWARD. So, then it really wouldn't matter if I stayed or left?

MONICA. Well, if you stayed I wouldn't talk about it anymore, but it's all I'd be thinking about.

HOWARD. Even if we made passionate love and ordered room service after?

MONICA. You want to?

HOWARD. Well, it's the most I've felt like it the whole time.

MONICA. Yeah?

HOWARD. Yeah, really, the only conflict I have is that if we didn't, then I could leave.

MONICA. That's right. You can leave. As long as you understand that if you do, the next time I see you, you will absolutely cease to exist.

(He considers it, then cordially points at her.)

HOWARD. I think that's fair.

(He exits. MONICA watches him go.)

(lights down)

SCENE TWO

(**SAM** *and* **GRACE**)

(A motel room, not the best one ever. **SAM** *and* **GRACE** *appear in the doorway and look around, nervously. Both in their early fifties,* **SAM** *is gentle and sensitive and carries a large, paper bag.* **GRACE** *thinks about God seventy percent of the day. Finally, she speaks.)*

GRACE. You think there's a Bible in the room?

SAM. I've never been here.

GRACE. Because I can't go through with this if there's a Bible in the room, or a ring on my finger.

*(***GRACE*** *takes the ring off of her finger, then opens up a night table drawer, then points.)*

Right there. Holy Bible.

(She picks it up and exits. **SAM** *considers the room, sits on the end of the bed, folds his hands in his lap, and reflects upon his entire life.)*

SAM. I knew I'd end up like this.

(He gets up and puts the bag on the counter. He takes off his shoes. And sits on the bed. He gets up and takes off his pants. He folds them neatly and sits back on the bed. He gets up and puts on his pants. He sits back on the bed. **GRACE** *enters, holding several bars of soap.)*

GRACE. I gave the Bible to Rosa from Paraguay who understood immediately why a person takes a Bible out of the room. *(shows him)* She gave me soap. She knows just enough English to let me know I'll be going right straight to Hell. *(notices)* You took off your shoes. Why did you take off your shoes?

SAM. *(innocently)* Grace, I only came and sat next to you at the movie because there was no one else sitting next to you.

GRACE. And I let you because I saw that you were separating your green Jujyfruits, and a man who does that needs to sit next to somebody.

(She sits by him on the bed, not too close. They just stare out a moment, neither having any idea what to do.)

Sam, have you ever done anything like this before?

SAM. I've never cheated on my wife, ever. Although I rarely think about anything else.

GRACE. What's held you back?

SAM. I'm afraid I'll get caught. Because I'm one of those guys who gets caught. When God made me He said, "Okay, this one will live a long time, but let he gets caught at everything."

GRACE. Sam?

SAM. Yeah?

GRACE. If we've been good people all of our lives, how much would this change us?

SAM. I think good people deserve happiness, don't you?

(SAM gently puts an arm around her.)

GRACE. Nnnggh.

SAM. *(removes his arm)* Hey, you want to have something to eat first?

GRACE. *(relieved)* Yeah. *(smiles at him)* You should at least buy me some dinner.

(SAM moves to the bag and takes out a barrel of KFC and a six-pack of Mountain Dew, and puts it on the bed.)

Maybe there's something on the television.

(GRACE picks up a remote control and pushes a button. We hear male and female moaning. Shock turns to utter fascination as they watch intently and eat chicken.)

(The moans reach a towering crescendo, and subside. SAM picks up the remote control and turns off the set. They sit for a moment.)

GRACE. So, that's how it's done.

SAM. Well, those are professionals.

GRACE. Yeah? I hope you're not expecting professional. Because I didn't recognize anything those people were doing.

SAM. When I was in high school, I only had one girlfriend. Her name was Martha.

(GRACE throws a pillow against the headboard, kicks off her shoes, grabs a piece of chicken and begins to appear a little more comfortable. She eats and watches SAM, attentively.)

She had deep red hair, like fire. And she had this angora sweater, and when the wind blew, the leaves would stick on it and she'd let me pull them off of her wherever they were.

GRACE. Yes, we're diabolical like that.

SAM. One winter, we went sledding together. There was a hill in Donaldson Park and new snow. And I asked her to wear that sweater, and I didn't bring my sled, so there would be only her sled, and we'd have to lie on top of each other to go down the hill.

GRACE. See, you guys are less clever, but we like that you include us in your plans.

SAM. So, her sweater got soaked from the snow, and we went back to her house.

GRACE. And there was nobody home.

SAM. And we went up to her room. She started to take off the sweater, but she was having a little trouble with it –

GRACE. Oh, I love this girl.

SAM. So, I helped her take it off. And she let me. And her shirt underneath was wet and she let me take that off, too. She was standing in front of me without her clothes on, and she was shivering a little. She let herself be completely vulnerable in front of me. But she smiled at me, as if I'd know what to do next.

GRACE. What did you do?

SAM. I held her against me. But feeling her next to me threw off my whole sense of balance so when I tried to kiss her I think I missed most of her head.

GRACE. Yeah, I still get kissed like that.

SAM. Everything we did that day was awkward. But, we did everything. And I knew that this was my day of days, and nothing finer would ever happen for me in my life.

GRACE. Oh, I'm sure –

SAM. *(immediately)* No.

GRACE. Well, I guess because you were in love.

SAM. Martha and I began to have more romantic evenings together, and what was once awkward became, and I'm going to use a word here that I've never again had the occasion to use in regard to anything having to do with me… *(puts up his finger in anticipation of a fantastic word)* …good. It was the first time I was good at something, and Martha was going to be the only one to know. I just thought, before we grew up, before everyone started to know what they were doing, if I could just show one other person how good I was, maybe she'd tell the rest of the girls and then they would all know but they could never have me because I'd be with Martha forever. So, I took some girl to bed, which was easy, because I belonged to somebody else.

GRACE. And you got caught?

SAM. Oh, of course I got caught! Martha walked in on me.

GRACE. Oh no.

SAM. I looked up at her, I said, *(with a cheery sincerity)* "Hi! I'm doing this for you!" I never saw such a look of such complete disappointment except on my wife's face all of the time. I don't think Martha ever spoke to me again. And you know what? When I was in bed with the other girl, I was pretending she was Martha.

*(**GRACE** looks at him.)*

GRACE. The first time I ever went to bed with somebody, I was twenty years old. A boy from down the street. We grew up together, we went through high school together and we graduated. I always loved him but I never did anything about it and he was gone. During the summer of my sophomore year of college, I was home and he was home, so, I had this plan that would make him realize that he had always loved me, too. I walked to his house and I went up to his bedroom and I stood in the doorway and I made this up: *(sings)* "Somebody loves you. Somebody good. Just say the word, and I would."

SAM. I would have been all yours for the rest of my life.

GRACE. Before I even finished the song he ran over and started to kiss me. Which I thought was so romantic because he wouldn't stop kissing me. And he kept kissing me while he took off my clothes, and I was having the moment that I always dreamed of right until I realized he was just doing whatever he could to get me to stop singing.

SAM. Did you ever see him again?

GRACE. *(nods)* I married him. Yeah, he's my husband. He's there every day. Uh-huh. *(looks at him)* Sam, if I go to bed with you, are you going to pretend I'm your wife?

SAM. Are you kidding? When I go to bed with my wife, I pretend she's Martha. I should be married to Martha. My children should look like us.

GRACE. You never heard from her again?

SAM. Once I got this letter with no return address. It said, "Sam, I'm married now, and I love my husband. And sometimes when the lights are out, and I love him the most...I remember you.

GRACE. You must have been devastated.

SAM. I was thrilled. Because as hard as I try, I don't seem to be able to satisfy my wife. But, without trying at all, without even being there, somebody thinks I'm terrific.

(He sips his Mountain Dew. GRACE kisses him on the cheek and looks straight out.)

GRACE. I think you're terrific, Sam.

(She gets out of bed.)

SAM. *(looks at her)* We're not going to do this, are we?

GRACE. What for? How could we possibly have had a better time?

SAM. Grace, I'm telling you. You don't want to miss this.

GRACE. I believe you, Sam. In my mind I'm fantasizing about your raw animal power and making love to me with such hungry passion for an hour and a half and for most of the time you've got me completely lifted off of the bed. And then you do it again. That's what's in my mind.

(They regard each other.)

SAM. Walk you to your car?

GRACE. *(smiles)* That would be nice.

(They exit.)

(lights down)

SCENE THREE

(**ALLEN** *and* **MICHELLE**)

(*An Upper West Side studio apartment. Same evening.*)

(**MICHELLE**, *early twenties, bursts into the apartment, returning from a wedding, looking fabulous. She is followed into the apartment by* **ALLEN**, *also early twenties, also looking at the top of his game.*)

MICHELLE. *(taking off her dress)* I always knew my life would be a collection of hideous moments ever since my mother told me I would never be a ballerina, which was difficult for both of us, but I knew... *(holds up a finger, confidently)* she was *right*. I accept that when God made me He did not dip into the reservoir of physical grace. But I've always tried to compensate for that with my own little personal charm which has somehow managed to keep me from some horrible moment of public shame until tonight! *(throws on some adorable night clothes)* You *did* it. You are now responsible for the most humiliating moment of my life! All this time I was sure it would be my Daddy. But it wasn't. It was *you.*

(she pulls out the bed from the couch)

ALLEN. It's a dead tradition, Michelle. It doesn't mean anything.

MICHELLE. It's not dead if it means something to me.

ALLEN. Yes, but if you'd *let* it be dead then we could go to sleep and so could the people next door.

MICHELLE. Oh, am I a little *loud?*

VOICE FROM THE NEXT APARTMENT. Yes, you are, Darling.

MICHELLE. *(to the voice)* Well, we're having a fight in here!

VOICE FROM THE NEXT APARTMENT. You go ahead, Sweetheart. I'm up now.

ALLEN. I don't even know what you're upset about. It was just a bunch of flowers.

MICHELLE. It was the bridal bouquet, Allen. And she threw it to me because she's my friend and all we ever talked about growing up was that we wanted our children to be friends, too.

ALLEN. You believe our getting married depended on you catching those flowers tonight?

MICHELLE. Don't turn this into a moment I can understand! Isolating the single women at a social function so everybody can think, "Oh, here's the big bunch of girls nobody wants," and then *throwing* something at them is not a moment anybody who participates in that understands. So get that out of here!

ALLEN. Then why did you join them?

MICHELLE. Because it was fixed. Because she was throwing the flowers to me and I was going to catch them. I was going to leap up in the air like it was *Swan Lake* and no matter what, I was coming down with 'em and it was going to be my one, true, graceful moment. And you were going to be standing there with this smile on your face like, "What a dope." And I was going to give you a kiss. And that kiss was going to tell you that I was yours for the rest of my life. And you were going to hold onto me way longer than appropriate and everybody there was going to think it was the sickest moment ever. Except for me and my friend in the wedding dress, because we could keep believing our wonderful thought about the children we don't have yet.

ALLEN. It was a reflex action, Michelle. I saw the flowers coming, I reached out and grabbed them.

MICHELLE. You climbed on a table and threw yourself six feet in the air.

ALLEN. *(proud)* It was the most spectacular catch in the whole history of men catching!

MICHELLE. It was the lowest moment of my life.

ALLEN. Because I caught the bridal bouquet?

MICHELLE Because you threw it back.

VOICE FROM THE NEXT APARTMENT. You bastard.

MICHELLE. Is there something wrong with me?

ALLEN. No.

MICHELLE. Do you secretly want a ballerina? Which I will *never* tell my daughter she won't be. Even if she only has one leg.

ALLEN. Michelle. To me you are a ballerina.

(That stops everything.)

MICHELLE. Boy, see, if we weren't having this argument I would just be kissing everything.

ALLEN. And I would let you.

VOICE FROM THE NEXT APARTMENT. And so would I.

ALLEN. *(turns to the wall)* You have to stop listening now.

VOICE FROM THE NEXT APARTMENT. I have nothing else.

ALLEN. *(turns)* Make me understand why we should change a relationship that works in a time when nobody's getting married anymore anyway.

MICHELLE. My friend just got married tonight.

ALLEN. So, because you are in the glow of an aberrant temporary corruption, this relationship has to be scrutinized?

MICHELLE. This relationship works because one of us believed it was *heading* somewhere. Now that I know you're not thinking that way, I think it's going to start not working so good anymore. ·

ALLEN. *(realizes)* I hurt us. *(looks at her)* I love you.

MICHELLE. No. You can't do both at the same time. Make a decision, Allen. You either love me or you're going to hurt me. And don't say 'I love you' anymore unless you really do.

ALLEN. I can't love you without marrying you?

MICHELLE. I'm not asking you to marry me. I'm asking for you to decide what I really am to you. I have. I would really give myself to you.

ALLEN. Why?

MICHELLE. Because I think you're the best person I know.

ALLEN. I caught your bridal bouquet.

MICHELLE. Pretty funny if it wasn't done to me.

ALLEN. What if you meet someone better?

MICHELLE. I'm trying to tell you that I'm willing to stop looking. Here.

(She takes his hands and puts them all over her body.)

All this can be yours if you call within the next twenty-four hours. Operators are standing by.

(She gives him back his hands and begins to get dressed.)

ALLEN. (stirred up) Wait. What are you doing?

MICHELLE. I'm teasing you. It's a big part of women ending up with the man they want. Pretty awful, but you can't ignore the history. Just like all this time you've been teasing me. I'm serious. You've got one day. Anything besides a "yes" is a "no".

ALLEN. (raises his hand) May I express my fear?

MICHELLE. (arms folded) I'm wide open.

ALLEN. I'm not saying it won't be a "yes," but what if there was something besides a "yes" that was above "maybe," like, "conceivable without actually being immediately so". Because that would not create what I feel "yes" would turn us into, which would be an out of control bullet train stopping only at the towns of "I do," "Twins? Huh." and "Gee, he died so suddenly".

MICHELLE. I'm the prize, Allen.

ALLEN. Too cryptic.

MICHELLE. I'm the prize. That's how my father loves me. Shouldn't you make me feel like that, too? And you're not supposed to catch the flowers. I am. They're for me.

ALLEN. You'd really leave?

MICHELLE. I'd really stay.

(She moves to the door.)

ALLEN. So, where are you going?

MICHELLE. Home. Now that I know this isn't, anymore.

*(She exits. The door closes. **ALLEN** stands. There's a knocking on the wall from the next apartment.)*

VOICE FROM THE NEXT APARTMENT. Hey. C'mere.

*(**ALLEN** crosses to the wall.)*

Are you here?

ALLEN. Yeah.

VOICE FROM THE NEXT APARTMENT. Okay, pretend I have my arm around you, Sweetheart.

*(**ALLEN** leans against the wall for comfort. He stands there.)*

VOICE FROM THE NEXT APARTMENT. This is very nice.

(lights down)

SCENE FOUR

(A modest house in Elizabeth, New Jersey.)

(GRACE enters in a hurry. She pulls a robe over what she's wearing. We hear the sound of a car pulling up. Headlights move across the windows. GRACE, not in her usual evening pajamas, desperately covers herself with a giant afghan she has been knitting for twenty years. She grabs the knitting needles and resumes her work on it. HOWARD enters.)

GRACE. How was your poker game, Howard?

HOWARD. I left just before I got killed.

(They consider each other.)

HOWARD. So, what are you working on? That thing?

GRACE. Yeah.

HOWARD. *(nods)* How long you been working on that thing?

GRACE. Twenty years.

HOWARD. *(nods)* What is that thing?

GRACE. *(realizes)* You're trying to talk to me, aren't you?

HOWARD. I don't know what I'm doing. These are just the particular words coming out.

(They nod their heads at each other, and the conversation ends. Then we hear the sound of keys in the front door.)

GRACE. Howard! Someone's trying to get in the door!

(He puts up his hand to motion GRACE to calm down. He grabs one of her knitting needles. He stealthily walks to the front door. Again there is the jiggling of a key in the lock. He disappears stealthily into the closet. The door opens. MICHELLE enters.)

GRACE. Michelle?

MICHELLE. Mom?

GRACE. Howard. It's Michelle.

(HOWARD enters nonchalantly from the closet and points the knitting needle at her.)

HOWARD. Michelle. You scared your mother half to death.

GRACE. What happened, Shelly? Is there a problem with you and Allen?

HOWARD. Did he do something to you? I will *end* him.

MICHELLE. We need to decide whether to get married or not see each other anymore.

HOWARD. You can't think about being married to someone and not seeing them anymore at the same time.

GRACE. Sure you can.

MICHELLE. Those are my choices.

HOWARD. *(to GRACE)* Do you understand this?

GRACE. Completely.

HOWARD. *(to MICHELLE)* You care about this guy?

MICHELLE. I'm living with him.

HOWARD. I hate that, by the way.

MICHELLE. I understand.

HOWARD. Then make me understand why you're here in the middle of the night.

MICHELLE. Because I can't stand him.

HOWARD. But you'd be married to him.

MICHELLE. *(angrily)* Yes!

HOWARD. *(to GRACE)* Do you understand this?

GRACE. Completely.

HOWARD. I want a son!

GRACE. Not tonight!

(**HOWARD** *exits.*)

(**GRACE** *looks at* **MICHELLE**, *and holds her close.*)

(*lights down left, lights up right*)

SCENE FIVE

(An upscale house)

(SAM is sitting on a couch, alone. He hears keys in the front door.)

SAM. *(calmly)* Hello? Who's that? Please come in and kill me.

(ALLEN enters.)

ALLEN. Hi, Dad.

SAM. Allen? *(gets up and hugs him)* What are you doing here at this hour?

ALLEN. Don't I still have a room here?

(MONICA enters in a flowing robe.)

MONICA. Yes you do, Baby. And you're always welcome to use it. You look thin. Is she feeding you?

ALLEN. Hi, Mom.

MONICA. Hi, Honey.

ALLEN. That's a pretty robe.

MONICA. Do you like it?

ALLEN. Yeah. *(prompting his father)* Doesn't she look great in it?

SAM. She does. *(then)* When did I buy that for you?

MONICA. You didn't.

ALLEN. *(instinctively changing the subject)* So, how you all doing?

SAM. Where'd you *get* that robe?

ALLEN. You all doing okay?

MONICA. *(it was bought for her)* I bought it myself.

ALLEN. You all doing okay, or what?

SAM. *(suspiciously)* Well-I-don't-like-it-as-much-anymore.

ALLEN. *(drops the bomb to change the subject)* Michelle wants to marry me.

MONICA. Who would do that?

SAM. *(turns immediately)* Allen! That's great.

ALLEN. You think?

SAM. She's a wonderful girl.

ALLEN. Yeah. I came home to consider the idea. How do you know if you want somebody all of the time?

MONICA. You don't.

SAM. It's true. You don't all of the time. But *lots* of the time –

(**MONICA** *looks at him.*)

You don't either.

MONICA. You've been living together a year and a half. And you're happy. Why change happy?

SAM. For the better. Where would we be if we didn't get married?

MONICA. Where are we, Sam?

SAM. We're in our house. Talking to our son. Who we made. That's where we are. We're still here is where we are.

(**MONICA** *looks at him. She nods.*)

(to ALLEN) You be with Michelle.

ALLEN. She wants me to take the day and decide.

MONICA. You can't decide the rest of your life in one day.

SAM. Monica, why don't you make us all a pot of coffee? It's late, we're not thinking clearly. Instead of rushing our judgments, maybe we could have a family discussion. We haven't had one of those in a long time.

MONICA. I'm discussing my son's future. You want coffee, why can't you make it?

SAM. Monica, please. I'm saying, "please." This shows politeness and cordiality.

MONICA. I'm not finished talking to him, yet. By the time you make us coffee, everything will be decided and then you can talk to him all you want.

SAM. I'll tell you what. Get your ass in the kitchen, make us all a pot of coffee or I'll pick you up and throw you out of the fucking house.

(MONICA looks at him.)

MONICA. Okay, but only because part of me liked that.

(She turns and exits into the kitchen.)

ALLEN. Dad?

SAM. Allen, listen to me while your mother's confused by my sudden show of strength. We only have a minute before she realizes it'll never happen again.

ALLEN. *(smiles)* Go.

SAM. This girl loves you. No matter what you may think of your own indecision, girls at this age know how to love.

ALLEN. So, how do I know if I love her?

SAM. You don't have to know. Love is just a word we've attached to a feeling we don't understand until we're old enough to look back and wonder what the hell we did. *(turns)* Do you love me?

ALLEN. Yes. I do.

SAM. Why?

ALLEN. Because you've cared for me. You've seen to my well being.

SAM. Why I done that?

ALLEN. Because you love me.

SAM. Why?

ALLEN. Why?

SAM. *Why*, Allen?!

ALLEN. Because you're my father.

SAM. Right. I'm your father. We've got husbands and wives, we've got parents and children, and that's what we got. So, I dedicated myself to you. We've grown up together and you've made me proud. But I never chose you, Allen. You were given to me. You're not a choice I made that I can just get out of. But what if you were? What if I didn't know you and met you on the street? Would there be some kind of automatic pull between us that would make me want you to be my son? Or would I walk away from you and not give you a second thought?

(**ALLEN** *looks at him, a bit shaken at that.*)

SAM. But see, the doctor said, "This is your son, take him home." And I understood the relationship completely. But go out and choose somebody you should spend the rest of your life with? What kind of responsibility is that to give a person?

ALLEN. I've never thought about that.

SAM. I think about it all of the time. *(turns to him)* Allen, look what this girl has done. She's made herself vulnerable for you. Don't try to figure out if you love this girl right now. You don't. It takes a lifetime to love somebody. One night you'll wake up in a cold sweat about all of the pressures you have but because she's there, sleeping next to you, you're fine. You know you're fine.

ALLEN. That happened to you?

SAM. Not once. We're talking about you. What matters is that she's your friend and she respects you. You got that, so stop thinking. Son. If you value my opinion, and Allen, I've been there, marry her. Marry Martha.

ALLEN. Michelle.

SAM. It doesn't matter.

ALLEN. Dad, with all your experience, let me ask you something and I'll understand if you can't answer me.

SAM. I'll answer you.

ALLEN. If you had it all to do again, would you still marry Mom?

SAM. *Your* mom?

(MONICA enters with a tray of coffee.)

MONICA. Here's coffee. May I speak with my son, now?

SAM. *(to ALLEN)* Yes.

MONICA. *(misinterpreting)* Thank you.

SAM. *(to ALLEN)* Because it took both of us to make you. And I could never walk away from you.

(SAM exits. ALLEN looks after his father. MONICA watches them, curiously.)

(lights down right, lights up left)

SCENE SIX

(early morning)

*(**GRACE,** in the middle of making breakfast. She flips on a radio on the kitchen counter. **GRACE** sings quietly along with the following, comforted.)*

GOSPEL CHORUS.
YOU MUST REALIZE WHEN WAKING/
WHAT A DAY IS IN THE MAKING/
WHETHER IT BE WARM OR FROZEN/
ON THE PATH THAT YOU HAVE CHOSEN/
TO TROD/
SAY, THANKS A LOT, GOD.

ANNOUNCER. "Thanks a lot, God" is brought to you by the Archdiocese of New York and the new Cadillac Escalade.

(hard pounding Cadillac drum theme, leading to)

MINISTER. FREEZE SINNER!

*(**GRACE** freezes and looks, startled, at the radio.)*

Yes, I mean you! For is there truly one among you who can claim to be free of sin?

GRACE. *(to the radio)* Nothing happened.

MINISTER. Can you?!

GRACE. *(nervously)* We just ate chicken.

MINISTER. And if you pridefully pat yourself on the back because you have not sinned in your actions, then I ask you this: *(thunderously)* Are you clean in your mind?

GRACE. *(shakes her head)* Not really.

MINISTER. But lift up your head for there is hope for your salvation!

*(**GRACE** lifts up her head.)*

MINISTER. Today's message deals with the seventh commandment!

(HOWARD enters.)

Thou shalt not commit adultery!

(HOWARD exits.)

MINISTER. But there *is* a way to cleanse your mind, my brothers and sisters! There is a way to leap out of the lake of fire!

GRACE. *(shouts at the radio)* This is not about me! We were in the same room but nothing happened so this is not about me!

MINISTER. Pray for Grace.

(Absolutely stunned, she looks at the radio as if she has been directly spoken to by God.)

GRACE. *(wails)* I'm SORRY!!

(MICHELLE enters)

MICHELLE. Mom?

(Immediately shuts off the radio. Turns to MICHELLE.)

GRACE. *(meekly)* I'm sorry.

MICHELLE. About what?

GRACE. About you and Allen and Hell.

MICHELLE. *(nods)* Yeah, it is hell. I was in my old bed, in my old room. I was thinking of the good little girl I was. Mom, why wouldn't someone want me forever?

(HOWARD peeks into the kitchen. Now that the radio is off, he enters and pours himself some orange juice.)

HOWARD. He doesn't want you forever?

GRACE. No decisions have been made.

HOWARD. I will *end* him.

GRACE. Why do you keep saying that?

HOWARD. Because I know there's actually not much I can do about this except come on strong.

GRACE. Where is he, Michelle?

MICHELLE. Home, with his parents.

GRACE. How come we never talk about his parents?

HOWARD. *(puts up a finger, sagely)* Because no father of the girl –

MICHELLE. We've talked about them.

GRACE. But we've never really made much of an attempt to meet them.

HOWARD. *(puts up a finger sagely)* Because no father of the girl –

MICHELLE. His dad is wonderful. You'd love his dad.

GRACE. What about his mother?

MICHELLE. He has a mother.

GRACE. So, why haven't we met these people?

HOWARD. *(puts up a finger sagely)* Because no father of the girl –

(but this time they're listening)

– wants to meet the father of the boy who's been getting it for free.

MICHELLE. DADDY! *(slaps him on the shoulders)* That's what's important to you?!

HOWARD. That's what's important to *him!*

MICHELLE. How do you know?!

HOWARD. Where's the ring?

GRACE. Howard.

HOWARD. WHERE'S THE RING!

GRACE. HOWARD!

HOWARD. I WANT TO SEE THE RING! I DON'T SEE THE RING! I WANT TO SEE THE RING!

(He grabs GRACE's hand and holds it up. There's no ring on it, but he doesn't see that, because he's looking at his daughter.)

YOU SEE THE RING?! THE RING MEANS COMMITMENT!

(**GRACE** *looks at her hand and then straight out, terrified.*)

THE RING MEANS LOYALTY! THE RING MEANS TRUST! (**HOWARD** *looks at* **GRACE**'s *hand.*) WHERE THE HELL'S THE RING?!

GRACE. *(immediately)* I TOOK IT TO GET CLEANED!

HOWARD. You couldn't clean it here?

GRACE. THEY HAD TO ADJUST IT! MY FINGERS ARE GETTING FATTER!

HOWARD. What are you screaming about?

GRACE. I'VE GOT FAT FINGERS!

HOWARD. Let me see them.

(**GRACE** *shows him her fingers.*)

They're fine fingers, Grace.

GRACE. *(cries a little)* You think so?

HOWARD. Yeah, what are you crying about?

GRACE. You think I have fine fingers?

(*He takes her hand and kisses her fingers. He turns to* **MICHELLE.**)

HOWARD. You see how she treats the ring? Because when you get one you take care of it and everything it means to you. Because it's the most important thing you ever get.

GRACE. Where's yours?

HOWARD. In my underwear drawer.

GRACE. I'd like to see it.

HOWARD. You think I don't have it?

GRACE. I'd like to see it.

HOWARD. No. It stays right there because I look at it every day when I put on my underwear which is the most personal thing a man can do because when you look

at your wedding ring when you put on your underwear
the symbolism of that is I'm married so I'm covering
up my situation.

(**MICHELLE** *puts her hand over her face.*)

GRACE. I want to see the ring.

HOWARD. Me, too. Where is it?

GRACE. In my night table drawer, next to the Bible. *(eyes
slit)* Get it.

HOWARD. *(heads upstairs)* You're a good woman, Honey.

(*He exits.* **MICHELLE** *looks at* **GRACE.***)*

MICHELLE. What is *up* with you two?

GRACE. Ah, Michelle. How complex is your relationship
with Allen?

MICHELLE. More complex than it should be, really.

GRACE. You think? And you're not even married and you
have no children and you've known him a year and a
half. I know your father most of my life. One day, after
you've know a man most of your life, you'll come to
the cemetery, you'll bring me a flower, and you'll say,
(shakes her head, pitifully) "Ohh, Mommy, Mommy..."

(**HOWARD** *enters down the steps.*)

HOWARD. *(holds up the ring)* I got it. Look at that. The
symbol of our love. *(tries to recognize it)* I ain't seen this
in years.

GRACE. *(menacing)* Put it on.

HOWARD. Boy, I'm not sure if I could –

(**GRACE** *takes the ring and jams it onto his finger.*)

(pain) YOU'RE HURTING ME!

GRACE. Never take that off again.

HOWARD. I understand your position, Honey.

(*He looks at the ring. He flicks his hand, subconsciously.
The ring doesn't come off.*)

Yeah, that's on there good, now.

(He flicks his hand. The ring doesn't come off. He looks at it. He heads out of the kitchen. He flicks his hand. He exits.)

(MICHELLE *looks at her mother and shakes her head, pitifully.)*

MICHELLE. Ohh, Mommy, Mommy...

(GRACE *nods at her.)*

GRACE. Right.

(lights down left, lights up right)

SCENE SEVEN

(MONICA, ALLEN, SAM. *Breakfast.*)

MONICA. I'm glad you've heard what your father has to say.
   He's entitled to his opinion and it should be respected.

SAM. Thank you.

MONICA. Now you want to hear the truth?

ALLEN. You know the truth about relationships?

MONICA. I do, because I've lived this long.

ALLEN. Okay. What is it?

MONICA. We live this long. You want to know what kills a
   relationship? Antibiotics. You drop dead at forty-two
   like we used to, then you might as well be happy with
   whoever clubbed you over the head, because where
   are you going? But now we live and we live, and
   relationships are not expected to change? This is the
   most important decision you will ever make in your
   long life. You'd better be sure of what you're doing.
   How many serious relationships have you had?

ALLEN. One. You don't like Michelle?

MONICA. I like her fine. She's cooked some meals for you?

ALLEN. We cook together.

MONICA. Who cleans the apartment?

ALLEN. We do those things together because we love each
   other.

MONICA. Because she cooks and cleans with you does not
   mean she loves you. Maybe she loves cooking and
   cleaning. Bring her over. Let her do the house.

ALLEN. Hey!

MONICA. Hey!! You're going to give her the rest of your life
   because she'll feed it and wash it? Allen. If you love
   this girl then what's the difference what I say?

(SAM *enters*)

MONICA. Or what your father says?

SAM. I just got here, why is there conflict?

ALLEN. I came to you both to learn something.

MONICA. Well, then you've learned that you're not ready yet. Because I am the *worst* person you can come to with this.

ALLEN. You're my mother.

MONICA. Right. And whatever woman you leave me for damn well has to steal you from me.

ALLEN. That's what you want her to do?

MONICA. No. But she'll have to. And then I will plague her for it every day. And, like I said, I live a long time.

SAM. *(to ALLEN)* That right there, is equal in weight to everything I said to you. Let the girl go.

ALLEN. You're kidding, right?

SAM. *(spreads his arms out pitifully) Look at me!*

MONICA. You know, whenever I make an important decision, I weigh the pros and cons. You want to learn something? Say them out loud.

ALLEN. Example.

MONICA. Con: Marry this girl and you cut yourself off from the entire female population.

(ALLEN looks to SAM.)

SAM. You don't cut yourself off. The female population becomes one woman and once you make her feel that way she will give her life to you. It's a pro.

MONICA. Con: You're too young. Why waste your strength and vitality on one girl?

SAM. Because he's at the right age to grow up with his children. It's a pro.

MONICA. He can't afford to support a family.

SAM. So they'll know down as well as up and love each other more for it.

MONICA. Con!

SAM. Monica. My love. Shut up.

MONICA. *(turns to* **ALLEN***)* Allen, if you make this decision without at least considering my point of view, then I have nothing more to say to you.

(**SAM** *considers that.*)

SAM. Another pro, Allen.

MONICA. If he does marry her I don't want him to remember that you were for it and I wasn't.

SAM. Monica, this has nothing to do with what you want or what I want. Why do you always have to think about yourself?

MONICA. I must feel like someone needs to.

SAM. Oh, here it comes. *(as* **MONICA***)* I wear Chanel suits and shoes with red bottoms, but I would gladly shop on Lexington Avenue if only somebody would love me. Monica, we love you.

MONICA. Why?

SAM. *(stopped)* Why do I love you?

MONICA. Why, Sam?

(**ALLEN** *looks at him.*)

SAM. I was initially captivated by your patrician attitudes and strong sense of interior design.

MONICA. That's why you love me?

SAM. You're just so different than I am that I figured you were better than me and perhaps worth having.

ALLEN. *(to* **MONICA***)* He means that your differences have always complemented each other. *(He looks at his father.)* Right?

SAM. I said what I said.

MONICA. How can he take a step like this if he's unsure?

SAM. He's not unsure. He's taking us into consideration because that's the way he was brought up.

ALLEN. No, I'm unsure.

SAM. Doesn't Michelle make you happy?

ALLEN. I don't know.

SAM. What do you mean you don't know? How can you not know if you're happy?

ALLEN. Are you happy, Dad?

SAM. What do you mean by that?

ALLEN. Are you happy, Dad?

SAM. I'm as happy as I'm going to get!

   (**ALLEN** *and* **MONICA** *regard him.*)

   (lights down right, lights up left)

SCENE EIGHT

(HOWARD, GRACE *and* MICHELLE. *Their kitchen.*)

HOWARD. Look, maybe there *is* something to living with someone you might like to marry.

GRACE. *(turns, astounded)* What?

HOWARD. She knows him better than we do, so only she knows what's right.

(MICHELLE *looks at* GRACE.)

GRACE. *(to her husband)* What's come over you?

HOWARD. *(sighs, tiredly)* I don't know. After thirty years of living in a house with women, it occurs to me that maybe I should just provide for you and agree with you and finally have the good sense to just keep quiet and be the first one to die.

MICHELLE. *(moves to him)* Dad –

GRACE. *(stops her)* You let him be.

HOWARD. *(to* MICHELLE*)* So, don't worry about pleasing me or your mother. Because we brought you up. We taught you everything we know and we've always tried to tell you the truth.

MICHELLE. *(turns to her mother)* You told me I would never be a ballerina!

GRACE. *(arms immediately extend to receive her)* I know. I'm sorry. You won't. They hug each other.

HOWARD. But, I'll tell you this; they're as much to blame as we are for allowing this to come to this point. I don't like these people.

MICHELLE. You've never even met them.

HOWARD. You'd think they'd at least have the courtesy to invite us out to dinner. I mean, our kid sleeps with their kid.

(GRACE *and* MICHELLE *can only look at* HOWARD.)

Doesn't that entitle us to a dinner?!

(**HOWARD** *flicks his hand.* **MICHELLE** *looks at her mother.*)

GRACE. He's right.

MICHELLE. What?

GRACE. *(hands her a phone)* Get 'em over here.

MICHELLE. Really?

(**GRACE** *nods.* **MICHELLE** *takes the phone and dials.*)

HOWARD. That's right. Except we go there because why does everything always have to be expensive for me?

(lights up on **SAM, MONICA, ALLEN**)

(**ALLEN** *'s cell phone rings.*)

ALLEN. *(looks at it)* It's her.

MONICA. *(grabs phone)* Michelle! Darling! How are you?

MICHELLE. *(into phone)* I'm –

MONICA. *(into phone)* You know, we were just talking about you.

MICHELLE. *(into phone)* You were?

MONICA. *(into phone)* Endlessly.

(**ALLEN** *manages to take the phone back.*)

ALLEN. Hi.

MICHELLE. Hi. *(a beat, then)* Okay, awkward doesn't work with us. I miss you.

ALLEN. *(into phone)* I miss you, too. When can we see each other?

MICHELLE. *(into phone)* My parents want you guys to come over for dinner tonight. They think it might help if we all got together.

(**ALLEN** *looks at his mother and father.*)

ALLEN. *(into phone)* I'd actually rather just get married.

MICHELLE. *(into phone)* Maybe there's something we could learn from them. Maybe we could take advantage of their wisdom.

ALLEN. *(into phone)* Uh huh. Are you taking a really good look at them? I'm just asking.

MICHELLE. *(smiles; into phone)* So, we'll see you tonight?

(ALLEN turns to his parents.)

ALLEN. Michelle and her parents would like to have you and Dad over for dinner.

MONICA. Absolutely not! It's a sucker play! They're throwing out the net! She'll reel you in like a trout!

ALLEN. *(turns to SAM)* Dad?

MONICA. No, Sam. My hair is a mess, and I'm way too young for this. Tell them we can't come.

(SAM gets up and takes the phone from ALLEN.)

SAM. *(into phone)* Michelle?

MICHELLE. *(Warmly. Into phone)* Hi.

SAM. *(into phone)* We'd love to come.

(MONICA looks daggers at SAM.)

MICHELLE. *(into phone)* Oh good. My parents have wanted to meet you forever. How's seven o'clock?

SAM. *(into phone)* What can we bring?

MICHELLE. *(into phone)* Just bring yourselves and I'm sure that will be plenty!

(SAM smiles and gives the phone back to ALLEN. MONICA is still looking at him.)

SAM. *(to MONICA)* Why aren't you interested in meeting these people?

MONICA. Oh, because what could we possibly have in common?

ALLEN. *(into phone)* Yeah, this could be an evening we'll remember.

(ALLEN and MICHELLE consider that, hang up the phones, regard their parents, and −)

(Lights fade. The curtain falls.)

ACT TWO

SCENE ONE

(**HOWARD, GRACE, SAM, MONICA, ALLEN** *and* **MICHELLE. HOWARD** *and* **GRACE**'s *home.*)

(*In darkness, the doorbell rings.*)

(*Lights up, living room.* **MICHELLE** *enters, looking lovely.*)

MICHELLE. I've got it.

(*She opens the door, revealing* **ALLEN.** *He kisses her.*)

ALLEN. God bless us, everyone.

(*He enters, followed by his father.*)

SAM. Michelle. (*kisses her on the cheek and takes her hands*) I'm so happy to be here.

MONICA. (*offstage*) Lovely little garden. What are these, flowers?

(**SAM** *sighs and moves to the couch.* **MONICA** *enters. She's a little overdressed for the evening but certainly looks spectacular.*)

Michelle.

(*She and* **MICHELLE** *touch both cheeks.*)

Lovely little living room. What is this, quaint? This is what we'd have if we did quaint. (*turns back to* **MICHELLE**) But where are your mother and father? We are on time, aren't we? You did say seven?

MICHELLE. (*smiles*) Yes, you're right on time. My mom and dad are running a little late.

MONICA. Well, I'm sure we could come back. When can we do this again?

MICHELLE. They'll be right out. *(calls)* Mother!

GRACE. *(calls back, offstage)* I'll be right out, Dear.

(SAM, who is now sitting on the couch, perks up. He lifts his head like a dog who has caught scent of something on the wind. Could this possibly happen to him? He looks up to God, astonished that this could happen to him. GRACE enters and crosses downstage to MONICA. She does not see SAM.)

GRACE. Oh. You must be Allen's mother!

(SAM, however, sees GRACE. His body goes immediately limp and for a moment he has absolutely no idea what to do and tries to become the couch. Panicked and having lost muscular control, he then drizzles down the front of it.)

MONICA. *(offers her hand)* Monica. How nice to finally meet you.

(SAM drops to his knees but there is no hole to crawl into. He turns around, faces the couch and hunches over and becomes an ottoman. Then, thinking better of that, he makes a spectacular leap and vaults over the back of the couch.)

GRACE. *(takes MONICA's hand)* We should have done this long ago.

(SAM peeks his head over the back of the couch just to make sure this is actually happening.)

I'm Michelle's mother, Grace.

(It's happening. SAM disappears.)

ALLEN. *(turns)* Dad, this is Michelle's mother –

(but no one is there)

Dad?

GRACE. Allen! How are you?

(They embrace. The afghan is suddenly pulled behind the couch.)

But where's your father? Couldn't he make it?

MONICA. My husband? He's right over –

*(She turns. **SAM** is gone. She turns back to **ALLEN**.)*

Allen, where's your father?

*(With everyone looking away from the couch, **SAM** crawls out from behind it, covered by the afghan. A hand reaches out from under it, opens the front door, and the afghan crawls outside.)*

ALLEN. Wasn't he was just sitting on the couch?

*(**ALLEN** looks to the empty couch, and notices the open door.)*

Door's open. He must have gone out to the car for something. *(He moves to the door and looks outside.)* Dad?

MONICA. Do you see anything?

ALLEN. *(squints into the darkness)* No, it's dark. Wait, what is that? There's like an aardvark trying to get across the street.

*(**ALLEN** shuts the door. **HOWARD** enters. **MONICA**'s back is turned.)*

HOWARD. Hi, everybody! Sorry I'm –

*(**MONICA** turns. They are nose to nose, one inch apart.)*

HOWARD. HAHHH!*!*

MONICA. *(breaks into a smile)* Oh, yay!

(Everything stops. And then, just between them.)

HOWARD. *(sotto)* What the fuck-ass-hell are you doing here?

*(**MONICA** breaks into a smile at the evening's sudden new potential.)*

MONICA. Well, I've come to your house, haven't I?

HOWARD. *(sotto)* You can't kill me now. I've got company.

MONICA. Howard –

HOWARD. Now is simply not a good time.

MONICA. I'm the company.

(HOWARD *doesn't immediately understand that.*)

HOWARD. I don't immediately understand that.

MONICA. This is my son, Allen.

(HOWARD*'s worst possible realization.*)

MONICA. *(smiles)* Congratulations. The world just ended.

(HOWARD, *a zombie, moves to* ALLEN.)

HOWARD. *(To* ALLEN. *Gestures to* MONICA.*)* You see that?

ALLEN. Yeah.

HOWARD. What is that?

ALLEN. That's my mother.

HOWARD. You're sure?

ALLEN. Pretty sure, yeah.

GRACE. Howard, this is Monica. Monica, this is my husband, Howard.

(HOWARD *offers a broad, toothy smile.*)

HOWARD. How are you? *(he sticks out his hand)* My name is Howard. This is where I live. *(realizes)* You know where I live now. This is Michelle. She's my daughter and I am the father of her. And this is my wife –

MONICA. *(with a lilt)* Mrs. Howard Janowitz.

HOWARD. *(helplessly)* Oh, God.

MONICA. *(looking at* HOWARD*)* But, it can't be Janowitz, can it? Because your daughter is Michelle Gerber, isn't she? So, Janowitz isn't anybody's name at all. Your name is Howard Gerber and I know where you live. *(looks at* HOWARD*)* Hey, that's quite a grip you've got on my hand there, big boy.

(HOWARD *lets her go. The doorbell rings.*)

Well, I guess my husband's decided there's nothing left to do but to join us.

GRACE. Well then we should let him in right now!

*(She opens the door. **SAM** stands there, wrapped in the afghan. He waves.)*

HAHGGHH!

SAM. I *KNOW!*

*(**GRACE** slams the door immediately and spins against it to face everybody while keeping her weight against it so it stays closed. Everyone looks at her.)*

(one attempt to keep it together) Dinner will be served right *now* in the main dining room.

*(**SAM** pushes the door open a little but **GRACE** slams it closed with her rear end.)*

GRACE. *(coming apart)* Right *now!* *(She sweeps both arms across her body and points her fingers like she was directing all of the airplanes to go to the dining room.)* Dinner will be served over there. Go *there!* *(the doorbell rings)* NOBODY'S HOME, ARE YOU *CRAZY?!*

MONICA. Grace. That's my husband.

GRACE. *(laughs nervously)* No. It isn't.

MONICA. It is.

GRACE. It's *not!* You know who that is? That's our crazy neighbor, Maurice. *(importantly)* He's crazy.

(the doorbell rings)

And you know what he's *fascinated* with?

(the doorbell rings)

The doorbell! That's right, "ding-dong". "Ding-dong, Maurice!" *(suddenly barks)* MAURICE! GO BACK TO CANADA!

MONICA. Grace, I think you'll find, if you open the door, it will be my husband.

*(**GRACE** realizes that she has put up the good fight, and there is nothing else to be done.)*

GRACE. Okay.

*(**GRACE** turns and opens the door. **SAM** is standing there.)*

GRACE. *(cont.)* This guy?

MONICA. Yes.

GRACE. Is your husband?

MONICA. Yes.

> (**GRACE** *nods three times, slams the door on him, and resumes her position leaning against the door. She folds her arms and looks up to God.*)

GRACE. *(to God)* Good one.

> (**MONICA** *moves to* **GRACE** *and takes exactly the same position next to her. She reasons with her, calmly.*)

MONICA. You know, I applaud your preoccupation with security. I do. And I understand there can be a lot of tension in an evening like this. So, although I only know you for five minutes, I feel I must ask, for the sake of the children…what the hell are you doing?

> (**GRACE** *looks at* **MICHELLE** *and* **ALLEN**. *They stand with their hands covering their faces in horror.*)

> (**MICHELLE** *slides her hand from her mouth.*)

MICHELLE. Mommy?

GRACE. Pray for Grace.

MONICA. *(to* **GRACE***)* Big decisions. Big decisions will be made this evening. But only if you open the door.

HOWARD. GRACE!

GRACE. *(immediately growls back at him)* NNNgggh!

> (*But having no way around this,* **GRACE** *finally turns to the door.*)

Yea! Though I walk through the valley of the shadow of death…

> (*In one motion she opens the door and hides behind it.* **SAM** *takes a step in.* **GRACE** *swings the door shut and is now standing next to* **SAM**. *They both stare straight out.*)

> (**HOWARD** *looks at* **SAM**, *standing next to* **GRACE**, *in shock.*)

HOWARD. *(aside to* MONICA*)* That's your husband?

MONICA. Yes, it is.

HOWARD. *(nods)* Well you got what you deserve.

MONICA. You're one to knock him, boy.

HOWARD. Who's knocking him? I pity the poor bastard. Look what you did to him.

(SAM and GRACE stand, catatonic.)

MONICA. Sam. I don't believe you've been introduced to Michelle's mother and father. You're standing next to Grace.

SAM. How very nice to meet you for the first time ever.

MONICA. And I'm here with –

(MONICA looks at him.)

HOWARD. Howard Gerber.

MONICA. *(smiles)* Of course.

GRACE. Well. Now everybody knows everybody.

(The adults all chuckle at that. ALLEN moves to MICHELLE.)

ALLEN. *(brightly)* So, how d'ya think it's going?

MICHELLE. Do something!

ALLEN. *You* have to do something. It's your house.

MICHELLE. *(turns)* Would anyone care for a drink?

(HOWARD, GRACE and SAM out of panic, MONICA because she'd like a drink:)

HOWARD, MONICA, GRACE, SAM. YES!!

HOWARD. *(to MICHELLE)* Fine idea, Honey. What can I get you?

MICHELLE. White wine for us, please, Daddy.

HOWARD. Grace?

GRACE. What?

HOWARD. Drink?

GRACE. I do now.

HOWARD. Monica?

MONICA. I'll have the usual.

> (**MONICA** *and* **HOWARD** *laugh at that.* **MONICA**, *delightedly.* **HOWARD**, *nervously.*)

MONICA. C'mon. Guess.

HOWARD. *(doesn't want to play)* But, how could I possibly know what that would be, crazylady?

MONICA. *(smiles)* Tanqueray Martini, straight up, extra dry *(She twists the skin on his arm.)* with a twist.

HOWARD. Sam?

SAM. Yeah.

HOWARD. What are you drinking, Buddy?

SAM. Scotch.

HOWARD. How about a double?

SAM. How about a bottle?

HOWARD. *(sympathetically)* Who could possibly blame you?

MONICA. Tell you what, Howard. Why don't I help you make the drinks? And your wife can take my family on a little tour of your little house.

ALLEN. Actually, Michelle and I have a lot to talk about, so we're going to step outside.

MICHELLE. *(smiles)* You want to step outside?

ALLEN. *(smiles)* Yeah, I really do.

> *(she escorts him out of the room)*

MICHELLE. *(turns to* **GRACE***)* Mom, we'll check dinner. You show Allen's father around. You'll love him.

GRACE. *(immediately)* What a thing to say! What an incredibly odd thing to...say.

> (**ALLEN** *and* **MICHELLE** *exit.* **SAM** *extends his hand. She looks at it and takes it and they head out of the room. Both of the men and both of the women regard each other as they pass.* **SAM** *and* **GRACE** *exit, leaving* **HOWARD** *and* **MONICA** *to confront each other.*)

MONICA. You never told me you had any children.

HOWARD. You told me your son was six years old.

MONICA. He was, once.

    (Turns to HOWARD *making drinks.)*

    How old are you, really?

HOWARD. Fifty-three.

MONICA. You're fifty-three years old?

HOWARD. *(hands her a drink)* Yeah. I'll be fifty-four two months ago.

MONICA. *(drinks)* I've been making it with a corpse.

HOWARD. Okay, seriously, how could you blame anybody for leaving you?

MONICA. You're not.

HOWARD. *(laughs)* Ohh, I am.

MONICA. No. I think you and I just had an off night and now is the perfect time to tell your wife you're leaving her for me.

HOWARD. Oh, yeah? Why is that?

MONICA. Because now she can see what a wonderful woman you're getting. And because if you don't, I want you to know that I now actually *have* come up with a way to end your life.

HOWARD. Monica, dammit, we don't like each other anymore. Why would you possibly want to keep this going?

MONICA. Because new clandestine relationships are a pain in the ass. You start losing track of what restaurant belongs to what guy. What guy likes what particular thing. What guy is which guy. Sam says, "What are you angry at me for?" And I'm not. I'm not angry at him. I just lost track of him.

    (They finish their drinks. HOWARD *pours them both another.)*

HOWARD. You're not angry at me either, Monica. You cocked-up your own life and you're the only one who can figure out how to find some happiness. That has nothing to do with me.

(MONICA sits in a chair and considers this.)

MONICA. I'm still killing you.

HOWARD. *(thought he got himself out of it)* Why?

MONICA. Because seeing your body lying there might give me two seconds worth of pleasure, which would be two seconds more than your body lying there has ever given me before.

(MONICA sips her drink as HOWARD picks up the New York Times from the counter, and pores through the headlines.)

HOWARD. *(impatiently)* Come *onnn!*

(lights down living room, lights up backyard)

SCENE TWO

(SAM and GRACE. The backyard.)

SAM. Grace!

GRACE. The trees in this yard are oak and poplar.

SAM. Last night was the sweetest night I can remember.

GRACE. For me, too, Sam. But we can't think about that now. What if the kids get married?

SAM. That would be fantastic! Things couldn't work out any better. Then it's all in the family.

GRACE. Is that incest?

SAM. Shh! No. It's not incest.

GRACE. Because this all stops at incest.

SAM. Grace, now we can have dinners together and see each other all of the time and it's okay! It's okay, Grace. Fate meant us all to be together.

GRACE. Last night was the sweetest night I've had in a long time. But I couldn't help wanting to hear those same words and feel the same feelings from my husband. You made me want to find him again. You're a dear man, Sam.

SAM. Grace, last night, feeling your care and your warmth made me feel something about my marriage, too.

GRACE. What?

SAM. I hate my wife.

GRACE. No, you don't.

SAM. I hate her guts.

GRACE. Why would you say that?

SAM. Because I live with her.

GRACE. Sam.

SAM. *(pitifully)* Because she hates me.

GRACE. No, she doesn't. And there's too much love in you to hate anybody.

SAM. And there's too much love in you not to have it returned. Let me return it, Grace.

GRACE. No. I'm not going through a life of the family seeing each other all of the time and knowing that we care about each other in secret.

SAM. Isn't that exciting to you?

GRACE. Yes.

SAM. Don't you want excitement in your life?

GRACE. No.

SAM. Why not?

GRACE. I'm not good at it. I don't want to know how to lie to my husband.

SAM. *(takes her hands)* You've given your life to your husband. What has he given you in return?

GRACE. The new Ford Taurus.

SAM. I had feelings last night. I want to have feelings. There's only one possible thing we can do.

GRACE. We should forget last night ever happened.

SAM. We should go to Tahiti.

GRACE. So, I'm way off.

SAM. Tahiti, Grace! Because without you I'll never get there! Waterfalls. Pounding sea. Cool lagoons. *(backing her around a tree)* You with flowers in your hair, in a sarong. Me bringing you piña coladas to your hammock. We have a little, thatched hut. You wear a coconut bra.

GRACE. No. This all stops at coconut bra.

SAM. Grace, why would you want to miss this? Grace! We could still be happy. Tahiti is happy.

GRACE. It's not reality.

SAM. Reality isn't happy! Forgetting last night happened isn't happy! Because it did. The reality is that it did.

GRACE. What do you think happened last night, Sam? Nothing happened.

SAM. That's why *everything* happened. You know what we had? We had true intimacy. Because without even touching each other we touched each other.

GRACE. *(absorbing that)* We had true intimacy.

(She moves to a little bench and sits.)

SAM. *(sits on the bench next to her)* You showed me I can still love somebody. I know what you deserve and I can give it to you.

GRACE. *(smiles at that)* What do I deserve?

*(**SAM** looks at her. Tentatively, he begins to sing.)*

SAM. *(sings)*
SOMEBODY LOVES YOU.

GRACE. *(startled)* Shh!

SAM. *(sings)*
SOMEBODY GOOD.

GRACE. You shouldn't do this.

SAM. *(sings)*
JUST SAY THE WORD, AND HE WOULD.

*(**GRACE** starts to sing with him.)*

SAM, GRACE. *(sing)*
SOMEBODY LOVES YOU. SOMEBODY GOOD.

(He gets up and offers his hand. She takes it and they dance.)

(sings)

JUST SAY THE WORD –

GRACE. *(sings)*
AND SHE WOULD –

SAM, GRACE. *(sings)*
JUST SAY THE WORD, AND WE WOULD.

(They continue to dance.)

(lights down backyard, lights up kitchen)

SCENE THREE

(**ALLEN** *and* **MICHELLE**. *The kitchen.*)

(*They regard each other silently for a few moments, then –*)

ALLEN. Okay, this is very hard to say.

MICHELLE. My parents are nuts out of their minds.

ALLEN.Mine too. Although, if you're keeping score, I think the most interesting point of the day belonged to my mother.

MICHELLE. Oh boy.

ALLEN. We live a long time, Michelle. I think you and I would have some very good years and have kids, and be distracted by the kids and then be fifty.

MICHELLE. Oh, please understand that this is good.

ALLEN. *(nods)* I understand what's good. What's good is when we're us. *They* were us. They were *us* once. Do they resemble us in any way now? What happens to us when we're *them?* When we're not as excited by each other anymore.

MICHELLE. *(smiles)* You will always be excited by me. You want me to prove it right now?

ALLEN. Do you think it's possible that people spend the greater part of their lives going crazy because they don't know what to do when they get tired of each other?

MICHELLE. You think our parents are going crazy?

(*Unnoticed by them,* **SAM** *and* **GRACE** *silently sing and dance their way across the kitchen windows and then out of view.*)

ALLEN. Yeah, I'm worried it's built into the deal. And I guess some people are lucky enough to get by it, but it seems like enough people don't to make me think that I would never want it to happen to us.

MICHELLE. That's what you've come to, Allen?

(HOWARD and MONICA enter, but ALLEN and MICHELLE are too absorbed to notice them. MONICA sips another drink, as HOWARD carries drinks for the others on a tray.)

ALLEN. What I've come to, whether you want to hear it from me or not, whether it takes a lifetime to know it or not, is that I love you, Michelle. I'd just like to know how you can marry somebody if you love them?

(HOWARD and MONICA react to that as MICHELLE arches her back, looks at the ceiling and covers her face with both hands. She stands like that until ALLEN moves to her.)

ALLEN. Shelly.

MICHELLE. *(her face covered)* You're going to let what you don't know is coming, get in the way of what you know we have now?

ALLEN. We do know it's coming. We watched it all day. What if we've inherited it? It's a fair question, Michelle. Shouldn't we consider what you and I might do to each other for the greater part of our lives?

HOWARD. *(to MICHELLE and ALLEN)* Wait a minute. I thought you were discussing this over dinner with mature adults.

MONICA. *(to MICHELLE and ALLEN)* Yeah. You know any?

(MICHELLE and ALLEN look at each other as GRACE and SAM enter.)

ALLEN. I understand that there would be easy parts. Our wedding day. The birthdays of our children. I understand we would be all over each other every night for the first five years.

HOWARD. Thanks for the image, kid.

ALLEN. But what about the hard part? What about the day that we don't remember we gave each other the best parts of our lives because we're too busy blaming each other for being two middle-aged potatoes.

GRACE. Oh, God.

(SAM immediately takes a drink from the tray. GRACE immediately extends her hand, and SAM gives her that drink and takes another.)

ALLEN. Michelle. Honesty can't hurt us. So, you make me see. You tell me what keeps us from crazy potato behavior for the rest of our lives!

(The parents all nonchalantly lean forward to hear this.)

MICHELLE. You're wrong about the easy part. The easiest thing we could do would be to smash this up and move on. But if we do, your little girl will never look like me. And when she meets her little boy it will never remind you of what we had together. That's how we'll remember the best parts of our lives. That's what will bring us back to *us.* You just have to trust us. You want me to tell you how not to go crazy *later?* You're crazy *now!* You have to tell me what's the matter with this girl, right now. There's so much to look forward to, Allen. And we've worked too hard to just be a memory.

(SAM is especially affected by that.)

SAM. Oh, God.

MICHELLE. *(emotionally)* And I would miss you for the rest of my life. I promise I'll do everything I can not to be too much of a potato.

ALLEN. Tell me why nobody wants to get married today.

MICHELLE. I don't know, maybe it's the end of the world.

(HOWARD and MONICA look at each other)

MICHELLE. *(looks helplessly at ALLEN)* Wouldn't you want us to be together for that?

(She doesn't want to break down in front of them. She turns and hurries out of the room.)

SAM. Allen. *(implores him)* Allen, please, go after her.

(HOWARD puts his hand on SAM's shoulder)

HOWARD. I think he has to do this by himself, buddy.

(**ALLEN** *stands, looking at both sets of parents. They look at him.*)

ALLEN. I have never, not ever, found one thing wrong with this girl. I don't care what she does to me.

(**ALLEN** *turns and exits after* **MICHELLE**. *The parents consider what just happened.*)

MONICA. *(drinking)* Well, I think my son is absolutely right.

SAM. *(suspiciously)* About what?

MONICA. I think honesty can't hurt us.

HOWARD. *(startled)* Sure it can.

(**GRACE,** *looking for distraction, grabs a platter of little hot dogs from the oven. She pours some mustard into a center dish.*)

GRACE. Would everyone like to start off with the little hot dogs? I made them because everybody likes those and I don't think anything bad has ever happened when you have them.

(*She holds out the platter.*)

MONICA. The four of us for example. How honest are we with each other?

GRACE. *(nervously starts eating little hot dogs)* Nngghh!

SAM, HOWARD. Monica!

(**SAM** *looks at* **HOWARD**.)

(*happy to pass it off*) Did you want to take this?

HOWARD. No, no. It's my house, so I spoke…but she's your wife, so –

(*He slaps* **SAM** *congenially on the sides of both shoulders and turns him around to face his wife.*)

– it's on you, buddy.

MONICA. I don't want to go through the rest of my life being thought of as a potato.

SAM. Nobody thinks of you as a potato.

MONICA. What do they think of me as?

(**SAM** *looks to* **HOWARD**.)

HOWARD. The thing that smashes the potato.

SAM. *(to* **HOWARD***)* It's like you're in my mind.

MONICA. But I do want to go through the rest of my life honestly. So, I don't want to talk about tonight anymore. I want to talk about last night.

GRACE. *(takes another hot dog)* Pray for Grace.

SAM. Monica, I want to talk to you right now.

MONICA. Go ahead, Sam.

SAM. Not here.

MONICA. Where?

SAM. Someplace private.

MONICA. The bedroom? Did you want to talk in the bedroom? Because that's really all we do in the bedroom isn't it? Talk. When we talk at all.

(**GRACE** *decides to eat the entire platter of little hot dogs.*)

We don't even kiss each other good night. I used to like that. It was hopeful. *(to* **SAM***, off of what* **ALLEN** *said)* Do you even remember that we gave each other the best parts of our lives?

SAM. I do remember.

MONICA. But when you stop kissing each other good night, maybe it becomes necessary to look elsewhere for hope. You know what I mean?

SAM, HOWARD, GRACE. No!

MONICA. What do you think I do when I'm not at home at night, Sam?

SAM. I try not to actually think about it anymore.

HOWARD. I think that's wise.

MONICA. *(to* **SAM***)* Why don't you think about it?

SAM. *(turns and looks at her)* Because it doesn't matter to me. It hasn't mattered for a long time.

HOWARD. *(to* MONICA*)* Okay? You asked your question, you got your answer.

MONICA. Well, it matters to me. It matters to me what went on last night.

*(*HOWARD*, doomed, covers his face with his hand.)*

MONICA. So why don't we just finally say what everybody already knows?

*(*GRACE *finally can't contain herself anymore.)*

GRACE. NOOO! It wasn't me! I wasn't with him!

MONICA. What?

*(*HOWARD *spreads his fingers apart to peek at what's going on.)*

SAM. I knew I'd get caught! Next time why don't I just print invitations!

GRACE. I was at home in front of the television! You know that, Howard! You know that! *(looks at him and shakes her head, pitifully)* I wasn't! Howard, I wasn't home! *(pathetically)* Pray for Grace.

(She eats a hot dog.)

HOWARD. *(drops his hand)* What the hell are you talking about?

MONICA. *(turns to* SAM*)* What the hell are you talking about?

SAM. I'm talking about me and Grace, what the hell are you talking about?

(everything stops)

MONICA. Well, I was talking about me and Howard, but fuck that, the news is elsewhere.

GRACE. *(absorbing it all)* Oh God.

HOWARD. *(absorbing it all)* Oh God.

SAM. *(absorbing it all)* Oh God.

*(*MONICA *watches, amused, as the faces change from shame to anger.)*

MONICA. *(amused) Here* we go!

GRACE. HOWARD! How COULD you?

HOWARD. How could *I?* How could *YOU?!*

GRACE. The same way you could!

MONICA. *(turns to* SAM*)* Since when could you?

SAM. *(blurts)* I could! And I'm *good* at it!

> *(*GRACE *takes the platter of hot dogs and storms off.* MONICA *follows her. She stops as she arrives at* HOWARD.*)*

MONICA. I just killed you. Have a nice day.

> *(*MONICA *exits after* GRACE. HOWARD *turns to* SAM. *They regard each other. They confront each other. They approach each other.)*

SAM. How long have you known my wife?

HOWARD. Biblically?

SAM. How long?

HOWARD. Eight months. How long have you?

SAM. One night.

HOWARD. Hardly seems fair. *(beat)* Did she have fun?

SAM. What?

HOWARD. Did my wife have fun?

SAM. We had a wonderful evening.

HOWARD. Good. That's good.

> *(*SAM *looks at him.)*

SAM. You're not angry?

HOWARD. Who am I supposed to be angry at? Her? She doesn't deserve whatever she wants? You? You seem like the sweetest guy alive.

SAM. All we did was talk to each other.

HOWARD. What?

SAM. That's all we did. She wouldn't let anything else happen.

HOWARD. *(nods)* And she continues to be a better person than me.

SAM. *(nods; then)* Are you in love with my wife?

HOWARD. *(laughs out loud)* Are you kidding me? *(then seriously)* No. Sorry.

SAM. *(disappointed)* Dammit.

HOWARD. It's over.

SAM. Yeah. I think for me, too.

HOWARD. You have feelings for Grace?

SAM. I want to take her to Tahiti.

HOWARD. *(smiles)* I probably shouldn't allow that. But go ahead, I'll give you three days.

SAM. *(smiles)* That's very civilized of you, but she doesn't want to go with me. We had conversation. We sang and danced. Then she told me she still wants all of that from you. She's loved you her whole life.

HOWARD. *(nods)* You would think that should be the simplest thing in the world to live with, wouldn't you?

SAM. I wouldn't know.

(lights down kitchen, lights up backyard)

SCENE FOUR

(the backyard)

*(**GRACE** and **MONICA** are sitting on the bench. The platter of hot dogs on their laps. They are deeply lost in thought, as they finish them. Finally **MONICA** speaks, in a reflective mood.)*

MONICA. We have a very precarious world situation.

GRACE. What?

MONICA. I'm sitting with you and I'm waiting for the world to end. I understand now, how you could reach a point when that's what you do. *(turns to **GRACE**)* But it won't. Because it's not the whole world that ends. It's only your world.

*(**GRACE** looks at her, wondering what should be said.)*

GRACE. I don't want that.

MONICA. No, you don't.

*(**HOWARD** enters, followed by **SAM**. **HOWARD** stands next to **GRACE**. **GRACE** looks at him.)*

HOWARD. It's the only time I've ever done anything like this. You'll never have to worry about me doing anything like it again. It's not the answer. The answer has always been understanding how lucky I am.

GRACE. What have I ever done that you could do this to me?

*(**HOWARD** takes a moment to wonder.)*

HOWARD. I'm sorry.

GRACE. I'm sorry, too.

*(She gets up, and exits. **HOWARD** helplessly turns to **SAM**.)*

SAM. You follow her, now.

(**HOWARD** *considers that, and then he does.* **SAM** *sits next to* **MONICA**. *They stay quiet for a moment.*)

MONICA. Why didn't you stop me?

SAM. *(softly, as he remembers from before)* Well, you're just so different than I am that I figured you were better than me and perhaps worth keeping.

(She considers that, and then, genuinely –)

MONICA. I'm sorry I couldn't make that last forever.

(They sit on the bench together. After a few moments, "Somebody Loves Me" begins to play. **HOWARD** *and* **GRACE** *enter and stand together.* **SAM** *and* **MONICA** *stand together.* **ALLEN** *and* **MICHELLE** *wheel out a trellis arch of flowers between their parents and stand underneath it. There are steps. The parents stand on one level, their children one level above.* **ALLEN** *hands* **MICHELLE** *a bridal bouquet.*)

ALLEN. "Whither thou goest, I will go; and where thou lodgest, I will lodge; thy people shall be my people, and thy God my God; Where thou diest, will I die, and there will I be buried."

MICHELLE. "I am my beloved's and my beloved is mine. When I found him whom my soul loveth: I held him and would not let him go. This is my beloved, and this is my friend. Rise up, my love, my fair one, and come away."

*(**ALLEN** and **MICHELLE** exchange wedding rings.* **HOWARD** *shows* **GRACE** *that his wedding ring is on his hand. The parents watch their children kiss, and then* **HOWARD** *and* **GRACE** *turn and head off.* **HOWARD** *puts his arm around her, and they exit together.*)

(Then **SAM** *and* **MONICA** *look at each other for a moment, separate, and exit in different directions.*)

*(**ALLEN** and **MICHELLE** come to the lip of the stage.* **MICHELLE** *holds up the bridal bouquet and smiles. She turns and tosses it in a high arc, into the audience.*)

(She turns and faces **ALLEN**. *They put their arms around each other, with every intention of holding on for the rest of their lives.)*

(lights fade)

The End

SAMUEL FRENCH STAFF

Nate Collins
President

Ken Dingledine
Director of Operations,
Vice President

Bruce Lazarus
Executive Director,
General Counsel

Rita Maté
Director of Finance

ACCOUNTING

Lori Thimsen | Director of Licensing Compliance
Nehal Kumar | Senior Accounting Associate
Josephine Messina | Accounts Payable
Helena Mezzina | Royalty Administration
Joe Garner | Royalty Administration
Jessica Zheng | Accounts Receivable
Andy Lian | Accounts Receivable
Zoe Qiu | Accounts Receivable
Charlie Sou | Accounting Associate
Joann Mannello | Orders Administrator

BUSINESS AFFAIRS

Lysna Marzani | Director of Business Affairs
Kathryn McCumber | Business Administrator

CUSTOMER SERVICE AND LICENSING

Brad Lohrenz | Director of Licensing Development
Fred Schnitzer | Business Development Manager
Laura Lindson | Licensing Services Manager
Kim Rogers | Professional Licensing Associate
Matthew Akers | Amateur Licensing Associate
Ashley Byrne | Amateur Licensing Associate
Glenn Halcomb | Amateur Licensing Associate
Derek Hassler | Amateur Licensing Associate
Jennifer Carter | Amateur Licensing Associate
Kelly McCready | Amateur Licensing Associate
Annette Storckman | Amateur Licensing Associate
Chris Lonstrup | Outgoing Information Specialist

EDITORIAL AND PUBLICATIONS

Amy Rose Marsh | Literary Manager
Ben Coleman | Editorial Associate
Gene Sweeney | Graphic Designer
David Geer | Publications Supervisor
Charlyn Brea | Publications Associate
Tyler Mullen | Publications Associate

MARKETING

Abbie Van Nostrand | Director of Corporate
Communications
Ryan Pointer | Marketing Manager
Courtney Kochuba | Marketing Associate

OPERATIONS

Joe Ferreira | Product Development Manager
Casey McLain | Operations Supervisor
Danielle Heckman | Office Coordinator, Reception

SAMUEL FRENCH BOOKSHOP (LOS ANGELES)

Joyce Mehess | Bookstore Manager
Cory DeLair | Bookstore Buyer
Jennifer Palumbo | Customer Service Associate
Sonya Wallace | Bookstore Associate
Tim Coultas | Bookstore Associate
Monté Patterson | Bookstore Associate
Robin Hushbeck | Bookstore Associate
Alfred Contreras | Shipping & Receiving

LONDON OFFICE

Felicity Barks | Rights & Contracts Associate
Steve Blacker | Bookshop Associate
David Bray | Customer Services Associate
Zena Choi | Professional Licensing Associate
Robert Cooke | Assistant Buyer
Stephanie Dawson | Amateur Licensing Associate
Simon Ellison | Retail Sales Manager
Jason Felix | Royalty Administration
Susan Griffiths | Amateur Licensing Associate
Robert Hamilton | Amateur Licensing Associate
Lucy Hume | Publications Manager
Nasir Khan | Management Accountant
Simon Magniti | Royalty Administration
Louise Mappley | Amateur Licensing Associate
James Nicolau | Despatch Associate
Martin Phillips | Librarian
Zubayed Rahman | Despatch Associate
Steve Sanderson | Royalty Administration Supervisor
Douglas Schatz | Acting Executive Director
Roger Sheppard | I.T. Manager
Geoffrey Skinner | Company Accountant
Peter Smith | Amateur Licensing Associate
Garry Spratley | Customer Service Manager
David Webster | UK Operations Director